An I Can Read Book®

# CAPTAIN CAT

## Story and pictures by
## SYD HOFF

**Harper**Collins*Publishers*

This book is a presentation of Newfield Publications, Inc.
Newfield Publications offers book clubs for children
from preschool through high school. For further
information write to: **Newfield Publications, Inc.,**
4343 Equity Drive, Columbus, Ohio 43228.

Published by arrangement with HarperCollins Publishers.
Newfield Publications is a federally registered
trademark of Newfield Publications, Inc.
I Can Read Book is a registered trademark
of HarperCollins Publishers.

Library of Congress Cataloging-in-Publication Data
Hoff, Syd.
    Captain Cat: story and pictures / by Syd Hoff.
        p. cm. — (An I can read book)
Summary: A cat makes friends with a soldier and learns about military
life when he joins the army.
    ISBN 0-06-020527-X.—ISBN 0-06-020528-8 (lib. bdg.)
    [1. Cats—Fiction. 2. United States. 3. Army—Fiction.]
I. Title. II. Series.
PZ7.H672Cap   1993                                          91-27518
[E]—dc20                                                         CIP
                                                                  AC

For Nina

Captain Cat joined the army.

He went in when nobody was looking.

7

The soldiers marched in a parade.

"Left, right—

left, right . . ."

Captain Cat kept in step.

He knew one foot from the other.

"That cat has more stripes

than we have,"

said a corporal to a sergeant.

"Meow," said Captain Cat.

Another sergeant looked at the cat.

"Yes sir!" he said and laughed.

From then on

everybody started saying,

"Here, Captain Cat,"

when they wanted him,

instead of

"Here, kitty kitty."

But sometimes the soldiers

had no time for Captain Cat.

"I have to clean the bathrooms,"
said one soldier.

"I have to sweep the grounds,"

said another soldier.

18

One soldier named Pete

always found time for Captain Cat,

even when he was on guard duty.

"You remind me of a cat back home,"

he said, and scratched Captain Cat

behind the ears.

Pete played with Captain Cat so much,

20

he got into trouble.

The general made Pete

do kitchen duty.

Captain Cat kept him company.

Pete let Captain Cat play

with the potato peels.

"Are you my buddy?"

asked Pete.

"Me-ow," said Captain Cat.

The next morning

a bugle blew.

Oh, how Pete hated to get up!

24

But Captain Cat

sprang right out of bed.

He had to check out the garbage

before it was taken away.

Then it was time for inspection.

Everybody lined up.

Captain Cat lined up, too.

The general fixed a soldier's gun.

He fixed Pete's hat.

All he could fix for Captain Cat

were his whiskers.

"Forward march!" said the general.